8 SHADES OF

Good Bye

By Lokesh Vishwakarma

SGSH Publications

SGSH PUBLICATIONS
Magathane Borivali East, Mumbai 400066
Email: sgshpublications@gmail.com
Website: www.sgshpublications.com

First Published by SGSH Publications 2024

First Edition: December, 2024
ISBN: 978-93-6631-364-1
MRP: 299 INR

TABLE OF CONTENTS

A HEARTBREAK'S TRANSFORMATION

A breakup isn't just a chapter ending; it's a seismic shift, a universe imploding and rebirthing. It's a rollercoaster of emotions, a whirlwind of confusion, a storm of grief. It's a silent war within yourself, a battle between hope and despair. It is an emotional quake that, if navigated with care, has the power to rebuild you into a stronger, wiser version of yourself as it was said in तैत्तरीयोपनषिद अंतः असूतिप्रारंभः or as Krishna Said in Shree Mad Bhagwat Geeta "आसक्तिः वेदना, करुणा क्रूरता, अन्तः आरम्भः।" means Attachment is pain, compassion is cruelty, and the end is the beginning.

This isn't just an emotional upheaval; it's a physical and mental battle. Your mind races, plagued by doubts and regrets. Your body feels heavy, your spirit weary. But remember, your worth isn't tied to someone else's love. You are a universe unto yourself, vast and infinite.

This book is your compass, your guide through this tumultuous journey. It will illuminate the path, help you navigate the storms, and emerge stronger, wiser, and more resilient. You'll learn to embrace the pain, to cherish the lessons, and to rewrite your story. So, let's embark on this transformative journey together. Let's face the darkness, embrace the light, and emerge as a phoenix rising from the ashes.

INTRODUCTION

It's too little too late...

"Trust is a huge burden! It weighs you down even while lifting you up".

Don't pour your tea into someone else cup of tea...You must know your cup.

The great irony or misery of ours we try to stay hungry and stay foolish.

Then you ask yourself "Where I went wrong? Which stone did you leave unturned? you tried to cover, you tried to compromise, you sacrificed, you talked, you listened, you got hurt, you gave love, you received pain, and you killed your inside life of to become someone's cup of tea. but it's too late & now everything you will do is too little too.

"Everything that counted doesn't count, and everything that counts is not countable."
As soon she has convinced herself that you had no future together. All of sudden you realized how valuable she is for you, and to your misery dear devil's advocates (usually BFF, roommate, or friend with one side fleeing for her) of her give her worst advice ever to break up with you. They, make sure that she could believe that it's better to move on.

Now all you can do is chase shadows of her,,,,,, but the question is how long???

"Your destiny delivers its most important messages in your loneliness". but you again realized it very late rather you get a wimpy ride of feelings which have 8 levels.

The Story

It had been an exhausting few weeks since Shiv and Shreya had been in constant disagreement on everything. they were not able to figure out from complete sync on thoughts how they became poles apart personalities. After a week of constant arguments, they finally decided to sit over and talk on this. They pinned a cafe at the side of lake Pichola, where they met for the first time 2 years back.

Shiv had a family business of antiques and art collections. Although he was not a big admirer of art and completely sees art and artefacts from a business point of view on the other hand Shreya is a big-time art lover, She also writes and loves to read. Shiv and Shreya met through art only. While driving to the cafe till reaching to the cafe shive was totally lost in his daydreaming about his first accidental meeting with shreya... Shiv entered the cafe just to grab his regular black coffee with cinnamon, while he was waiting for his coffee he noticed a beautiful card on the side table. He could not resist himself to check it. This card was addressed to "Miss Shreya Sahani" This was an invitation to an art exhibition going to help at City Place Udaipur on **July 13th**. The itinerary and craft details of that exhibition suddenly sparked a light in his business mind.

"Excuse me that belongs to me..." While Shiv was exploring the card an utterly sweet voice hit his ear drum...it was Shreya. In her ideates, elegance with off-white Anarkali, adorned with intricate designs and her long Jhumka completely complimented her dress. Shiv almost sunk into her big expressive eyes. Her delicate bindi on her forehead looks like जैसे

खूबसूरत शब्द में लगा नुख़्ता हो and a charming potli bag, embodying grace and creativity. Shiv was just staring at her with an open mouth...

Just to break the awkwardness Shreya said- Excuse me that's my invitation card...you also admire art?

Shiv just realised he was behaving like a nerd.. to make the situation normal he said..." Not admire but buyer...Hi I am Shiv Wadhawa I deal in antiques and artefacts.

Hi I am Shreya, Sahani just Art admirer, I think you should also visit this exhibition no!! you may find something which will add to your revenue a lot. Shreya smiled and took the card from his hand and left.

Now today after, 2 years they are seating across from each other in the dimly lit café, While the space between them thick with unspoken words. The air felt heavy, as though every breath they took carried the weight of everything they hadn't said, the things they'd tried to ignore. Their eyes met, but neither knew how to begin.

Shiv fiddled with his coffee cup, trying to summon the courage to speak. He could feel the ache in his chest—an emptiness that only grew with each passing second they sat in silence.

Finally, Shreya spoke, her voice softer than usual, almost as if she were trying to keep the walls she'd built around herself intact.

"Shiv, I think we both know things aren't the same anymore," she said, her eyes tracing the rim of her cup.

He looked at her, pain flashing in his eyes, and shook his head. "I don't want to believe that. Not yet. Not like this."

"I didn't want to either," she whispered, "but I'm tired of fighting for something that's already slipping away. It's like we've been holding on to the pieces of something that doesn't fit anymore."

Shiv felt his heart sink. He hadn't wanted to hear it, but somehow, he knew it was coming. They had fought so hard to keep this relationship alive, even when everything around them was crumbling. They fought against themselves, against each other, and against the distance that had started creeping in. But now, sitting in front of her, Shiv couldn't deny it any longer.

"I just don't understand," he said, his voice thick with emotion. "How did we get here, Shreya? It feels like one day we were fine, and the next... this." He gestured between them, the emptiness lingering in the space. "I thought we could make it through anything."

She looked up at him, her eyes filled with a sadness he hadn't seen in a long time. "We fought for it, Shiv. We did. But fighting isn't enough when it's like we've already lost what we had. We've been trying to hold onto a relationship that's already over."

Shiv shook his head, trying to fight the tears that burned in the back of his eyes. "But what about all the good times? What about the way we used to talk for hours, the way we laughed at the stupidest things? Doesn't that mean something?"

"It does," she said quietly. "But it's not enough to hold us together anymore. We're not the same people we were back then, and neither of us is happy pretending we are."

Shiv felt like the ground had been pulled out from under him. He had always thought they would work through everything, that no matter how messy things got, their love would survive. But now, as he looked at her—her face soft but distant, her eyes avoiding his—he couldn't help but feel the sharp, cold truth of it.

"But... Shreya, I love you. I love you so much," he said, his voice trembling. "I know things have been hard, but I swear, I can do better. We can do better. We just have to fight a little harder, don't we?"

She closed her eyes for a moment, as if weighing his words, then slowly shook her head. "I can't keep fighting, Shiv. I'm exhausted. It's not just about love anymore. I thought I could hold on, but I can't. It's like we're two people trying to hold on to something that's already slipping through our fingers."

He wanted to argue, to make her see how much he still needed her, how much he still believed in them. But the words felt useless now, like hollow echoes of a past that no longer existed. Instead, he fell into silence, looking at her with a mixture of disbelief and sorrow.

"You don't even see it, do you?" Shreya said, her voice quieter now. "I've been trying to get through to you for so long. I've been hoping you'd realize how much you've changed. How much we changed. I don't want to be the one who gives up first, but you've already stopped fighting for us, Shiv. You just don't see it."

Shiv's heart cracked open at her words. He opened his mouth to speak, but no words came out. The truth of what she was saying sunk in like a dagger, and he felt an overwhelming rush of guilt and regret.

"Shreya, I—" He stopped, unable to finish the sentence. He didn't know what to say. He didn't know how to fix this.

"You don't have to say anything," she said, her voice barely above a whisper. "I've been waiting for you to see it. But you never did."

The weight of her words hung in the air between them, suffocating any remaining hope.

"I thought you instinctively understood," he finally managed to say, the words feeling weak even as he spoke them. "That's why I never said it out loud. I thought you knew how much I loved you. How much I still do."

Shreya looked at him, her eyes filled with a sadness that was almost too much to bear. "I did, Shiv. I always knew. But knowing doesn't always make it enough. Sometimes, we need more than love. We need understanding, respect... we need to feel like we belong in each other's lives. And I haven't felt that in a long time."

His mind was racing. She was right, of course. They had both been lost in their own worlds, trying to hold on to a relationship that had long since passed its prime. He had been so wrapped up in his own insecurities and fears that he had stopped paying attention to the things that really mattered—the little things, the moments where love was supposed to be a choice, not just a feeling.

He didn't know how to fix it. But he knew one thing for sure: he couldn't lose her.
"I can't just walk away from this, Shreya," he said, his voice filled with desperation. "Please, don't do this. Please, don't say it's over."

She met his eyes, and for the first time in a long time, he saw the quiet resolve in her gaze. "Shiv... I'm not asking you to walk away. I'm just telling you that I can't keep waiting for something that's not going to change. I'm done pretending that we can fix something that's already broken."

Shiv looked at her, the weight of her words crashing down on him. His heart screamed at him to hold on, to fight for what they had, but deep down, he knew she was right. It wasn't just about love. It was about something deeper—something they had lost along the way.
He stood up, his body heavy, feeling the crushing realization that it was truly over.

"Okay," he whispered, his voice barely audible. "I give up."
Shreya stood as well, her eyes softening with sorrow. "I never wanted it to end like this, Shiv. But we've both been holding on to something that's already gone. I'm sorry."

And with that, she turned to leave, her footsteps fading into the distance, leaving Shiv standing in the silent emptiness of what was once a love he thought would never fade.

He stared at the door for a long time, as if willing her to come back, but deep inside, he knew she wouldn't. This is the beginning had already begun the beginning of the end. The level one of Break Up.

LEVEL ONE

The beginning That already begins....

The Beginning that begins when you were lost in yourself. We fought to ourselves or even every single person in between, to hold on the relationship to this point where it being all-consumed. Our brain and body don't want to believe it's actually; started to end. We can't believe it. Even if it was awfully blemished pair, even unbearable at many times, but the idea of getting single is unacceptable to you.

Someone near to your heart, the moment you realize that this person will not be available now onwards, You suddenly start feeling lonely, The guy who was the spark of all party, the guy who was full of life, full of him, suddenly became empty and vacant from inside just because you believed that she instinctively understand the unsaid...as you love her so much.

Now, just to have her attention, you begin to do all sorts of silly, foolish things, idiotic things- you change your DP, Status with other girls, wear a funky dress, eat out with friends or either behave oddly...watch meaningful movies, you talk philosophy some may relate to René Descartes's "Cogito ergo sum.." or stop talking...and so on.

After all the melodrama you finally starting to compute that it's over. we move from, "Don't leave me!" to "Okay, I give up." But you still feel anything but okay.

The moment you get off the phone with your ex, or the messaging finally stops, or you leave each other's space of routine life, you face withdrawal and are hit relentlessly by the reality of what you have lost. It can be a brutal process. it will take a long time, it's just level one until or unless you will not start to feel deserving of investing in your own independence and reshaping your life path it will remain utterly painful.

The Story Continues....

Shiv came to his hotel room sat on the edge of his bed, his mind racing. Every word Shreya said at Café was echoing in his head. The room felt suffocating, the silence deafening. The weight of the breakup had hit him harder than he expected. It wasn't just the loss of Shreya—it was the unbearable desperation to understand why. Shiv was desperately asking himself Why had they fallen apart. Why Shiv, why you hadn't seen the signs earlier? Why hadn't you fought harder?

The thoughts spiralled, each question feeding into the next, consuming him. There was an ache deep within, a gnawing need to make sense of the unravelling. Shiv could still hear Shreya's last words echoing in his mind: "We're not the same people anymore, Shiv." But how could that be? How could everything they shared the laughs, the quiet moments, the promises be gone?

Shiv tried to tell himself "It was over Shiv". The clarity would hit him at some point, right? But the fog of disbelief was thick, and his mind kept circling back to the same thing: What happened?

Shiv grabbed his phone and opened the messages from his best friend, Mayank, seeking comfort in the familiar faces. But even their words felt hollow, like they were trying to fill a hole too deep to reach.

"kya hua..? Tu mila Shreya se? Kya boli wo..." shiv couldn't revert "Dude, she's just being emotional. You guys can still make it work. She'll come around," in the next massage Mayank texted.

But Shiv knew deep down that it wasn't just about emotions. It wasn't that simple. He had loved her with everything he had, but love wasn't enough when the connection wasn't there anymore.

He scrolled through his contacts, stopping at a message from Shreya. The texts were mostly mundane, but then, he found a thread from months ago, a conversation where they had been laughing about something trivial. "We'll always figure things out," she had said then. "I'll always be here for you, no matter what."

Shiv's chest tightened. The contradiction of those words against the harsh reality now felt like a betrayal. Had she meant them? Did she even understand how much those words meant to him?

That's when the panic set in. Was it me? Was it something I did? His mind flooded with all the small things he could have done differently. He tried to fixate on something, anything that would explain the sudden silence between them. He thought of the late-night talks, the trips they had planned, the future they had once talked about with so much certainty.

But now, everything felt like a broken puzzle.

He jumped out of bed, unable to sit still, pacing around his apartment. His phone buzzed again. Another text. Another distraction.

"Bro, just move on. You know how Shreya is. She needs space. You've got to let her figure things out," this was Mayank again!!

Shiv wanted to scream. How could he just let it go? Was that the right thing to do? Was he supposed to just let her slip away, like everyone else who had faded from his life?

But that was it, wasn't it? He had spent so long chasing her, trying to win her over, to feel like he was enough. He had convinced himself that if he could just be what she needed, if he could just be there for her when no one else was, then everything would be fine.

Shiv had been addicted to the chase, the feeling of winning someone over, of making her believe that he was the one who could give her everything. It felt like a high, a rush of validation. But now, the dopamine had worn off. And with it, the rush of love had faded too.

He wasn't enough anymore, and that realization was sinking in. Shiv pulled up Shreya's Instagram, his eyes scanning her latest posts. She looked beautiful, as always—her big eyes shining, a soft smile on her lips. She had posted a picture of herself in the off-white anarkali, an outfit he had once told her looked perfect on her. The memory hit him like a wave, washing over everything else.

The desperation grew inside him. I can't lose her. I can't. But then the voice in his head told him that he wasn't just chasing her anymore. He was chasing an ideal—a version of love that had never truly existed. And in his desperation to fix things, he had lost sight of the reality that maybe it wasn't just about her. It was about him too. About what he had become in this relationship.

He sighed, sinking down onto the couch. Maybe I never understood it at all. His mind flashed to the words he had read just a few days ago. "Whatever is going on in our relationships is often a projection of the inside thought process of us."

Had Shreya really changed, or had he just seen the cracks through his own insecurities?

"Whatever happened, it's over," Shiv whispered to himself, but the words felt foreign. He wasn't ready to accept it, not yet.

As the days passed, the desperation only intensified. He found himself talking to friends, family, even strangers on social media, explaining why it didn't make sense, why the breakup shouldn't have happened. He argued, debated, tried to convince anyone who would listen that he could fix things that they could fix things.

But deep inside, Shiv knew the truth: No amount of arguing would bring back the past. No amount of justification would make her see that he still loved her. The problem wasn't just her; it was the way he had been chasing something elusive, believing that love was a game to win.

It wasn't until late one night, when he sat alone in his apartment, staring at the empty space where they once laughed together, that it finally hit him.

He had been playing the wrong game on a turf that wasn't meant for him. This wasn't a race to win. This was supposed to be a journey, with small goals, shared moments, and laughter along the way. Instead, he had turned it into a chase. A chase that had ultimately led him nowhere.

Shiv looked at his phone one last time, checking for any new messages from Shreya. There was nothing. And in that moment, he realized—this is what level two of a breakup feels like.

Desperation. Confusion. A need for closure that might never come. And the painful truth that he wasn't playing the right game all along.

He closed his eyes and whispered to the empty room, "I'll learn from this. Eventually. But for now... I need to let go." And he did. Their relationship reached at The Level Two which is summed up as follows-

LEVEL TWO

Desperation to have an ECO....

It is characteristic of wisdom not to do desperate things because life is a process by which a few desperate longings morph into a thousand meaningless wants. The wants that never goanna be fulfilled, never goanna to be satisfied. and never let yourself to be complete.

But the drive to know why it is happening at all; is consuming, killing, destroying at every level of thoughts. We must understand why this happened, maybe beyond anyone's ability to explain it and beyond your ability to digest but still, you must give a thought to it.

Do not just fixate on things your ex-said at various times that you see as contradicting the breakup, and you hold onto them now as if they are gospel.

"Whatever is going on in our relationships is often a projection of inside thought process of us"

Yet somewhere within, you have moments of clarity, too. You likely swing back and forth between foggy disbelief, the daily, moment-by-moment rediscovery of the magnitude of your loss, and flashes of painful clarity that of course, it's over. The pain, disorganization, and confusion can become all you think about, or talk about.

But initially, we remain driven to understand what happened, at any cost. The desperation to make sense of something so jarring compels you to debate friends, family, co-workers, even strangers, about why the relationship ended, while you justify to them the reasons it shouldn't have as if convincing them it is equal to convincing your ex.

The feeling of I has been knowing her/him for long. She/he is smart...independent...ambitious, and...with relationship status that consistently reads...'it's complicated'.

She/He doesn't realize but her/his problem is that 'she/he is forever attracted to someone who is hard to get for others, and if are blessed enough to have him/her, you must value him/her and if not, then this is how it goes: We find that 'someone', obsesses, pursues, and makes a chase out of it. And finally, we win. Congrats!!! But...'now what'? Well! Now, something goes missing. After all, when we started with the 'zenith', the road next only goes downhill. Now, with 'dopamine rush' gone, things get messed up...it's all lukewarm...and doesn't quite feel the way it is supposed to.

And sadly, we don't know that the problem is much bigger than we think. The problem is inside us.

The false feeling of achievement inside finding the wrong outlets. And the realm of relationships isn't the apt one for a '100-meter' race put on an infinite loop. It is supposed to be a golf game played for leisure, with many small goals, achieved one after another, on changing courses, with casual banters, unplanned laughs, pats on the back, high fives, occasional teasing and 'never mind, there is always next time' pronounced with a familiar accent.

Alas! I wish we could realize..."Dear Me, you are all the time playing the wrong game on a right turf.

And you know what? There is another thing I feel like whispering to me. And to my girl that is: "My life...let me also tell you a secret...'No man is even half as good as he seems while you are chasing him"

And remember one thing "Make your self-priority once in a while, it's not selfish its necessary. Don't lose respect to get attention."

If you can relate this write-up with yourself, then congratulations!!! Friend you are at level 2 of a break-up. expect a lot more disaster.....

The Story Continues....

Shiv sat in the balcony, staring out at the city lights below, his thoughts a tangled mess. His eyes were wet and red...The weight of the breakup felt heavier each day, a constant presence in his chest. It's over, the words echoed in his mind, but every time he tried to accept it, a new wave of desperation surged within him.

He couldn't shake off the idea that maybe, just maybe, there was still a chance. He said to himself... "Shiv ऐसा भी तो हो सकता है She is just punishing you or it just prank..."

The thought of losing Shreya, of never hearing her laugh again, of never holding her hand it was too much to bear. And so, like countless others before him, Shiv found himself bargaining.

I'll be better, he promised himself. I'll fix everything that went wrong. I'll change whatever she didn't like about me. I'll be the perfect version of myself for her. She'll see how much I love her. She'll come back.

His phone buzzed, and for a fleeting moment, his heart skipped a beat. It was a message from Shreya.

"Hi Shiv," it read, simple and cold, but it was enough to pull him back into the cycle. He quickly typed a response, his fingers trembling.

"Shreya, I know I've made mistakes. But I'll change, I swear. I'll be more attentive, more understanding. I won't take you for granted again. I love you, and I'll prove it to you. Please don't walk away from us."

He stared at the message for a long time, wondering if it was too much, too soon. But he couldn't help himself. The thought of never hearing from her again, of her moving on, was unbearable.

The moments that followed were a blur. He checked his phone obsessively, hoping for a reply, hoping that she'd acknowledge his words. But the response never came. The silence was crushing.

Shreya had been quiet for days now. Ever since the breakup, she had withdrawn, and Shiv couldn't stop himself from analysing every word, every gesture, every interaction they'd had. Maybe if he hadn't been so distracted with work, maybe if he'd paid more attention, maybe if he had just tried harder...

He found himself rethinking everything they had shared. Those late-night walks, those moments of comfort when their hands intertwined, the shared dreams of a future together. They had been so close, so real. How could it all just fall apart so easily?

As the days dragged on, Shiv tried to pull himself together. He started working out, changed his social media profile picture, began hanging out with friends more often—anything to distract himself from the ache inside. But none of it helped. It felt like he was trying to fill a void with fleeting distractions.

One evening, he called Mayank, his best friend, desperate for a sense of direction.

"Bro, I don't know what to do anymore," Shiv confessed. "I keep thinking about everything I could've done differently. I feel like if I can just fix it, if I can show her that I'm better… maybe she'll come back."

Mayank was quiet for a moment, before responding, "Shiv, you're bargaining with yourself. You can't change everything about you to fix what's broken. A relationship isn't about one person doing everything. You both contributed to how things ended. You can't carry the entire weight of it."

But Shiv wasn't ready to hear it. He wasn't ready to let go. He felt like if he could just fix his mistakes, he could undo the pain, rewind time, and make everything right again.

As he hung up the phone, he thought about Shreya's words "We're not the same people anymore." The phrase echoed in his mind, but it didn't make sense. How could they have changed so much, so quickly? What had gone wrong?

He texted Shreya again, his fingers almost numb with anticipation.

"Shreya, please. I'll do anything. Just give me a chance to show you that I can be the person you need. I've learned. I've changed. We can work this out, I know we can."

But as the minutes ticked by, and the silence grew longer, a sinking feeling began to grow inside him. What was he really doing?

Was this love? Or was it desperation? The more he bargained with her, the more he realized it wasn't really about what he could do for her anymore. It was about not accepting that it was truly over.

At night, lying in bed, Shiv replayed the good times they'd had—those moments where everything felt right. He tried to convince himself that it could still be salvaged. But deep down, a small voice told him the truth: You can't bargain your way back into someone's life.

And yet, the thought of her slipping away completely was unbearable. He wasn't ready to let go, not yet. He wasn't ready to admit that his attempts to fix everything, to change, to prove his love, were just temporary distractions from the reality he had to face.

Shreya was moving on. And no amount of bargaining could change that.

But Shiv couldn't stop himself. He was stuck in a cycle—one that promised to bring answers, but only deepened his confusion. The desperation to make things right, to get back what they had, kept him reaching for something that was slipping further out of reach.

As the night wore on, the weight of his own bargaining began to sink in. He wasn't just bargaining with Shreya he was bargaining with himself, hoping that by changing enough, by doing enough, he could control the outcome. But he couldn't.

And maybe, just maybe, he had to learn that letting go was the only way to move forward. Here Shiv and Shreya's Break up came to Level three "The Bargaining"

LEVEL THREE

The Bargaining

Unconditional love is a myth in the contemporary world. I remember a famous dialogue from super hit movie MOHABBATEIN.

"कोई प्यार करे तो तुमसे करे,

तुम जैसे हो वैसे करे,

तुमहे बदल कर जो प्यार करे,

वो प्यार नही सौदा करे, और

साहबिा प्यार में सौदा नही होता"

We have given a greats hand in the theatre while watching the movie on this particular dialogue because somewhere somehow everyone has been bargained for their love and even you have bargained, you negotiated then too most of us ended empty.

"न कर सके हम उनसे दलि का सौदा,

लूट के ले गए लोग हमे मोहबत का दलिासा दे कर"

While dealing with breakup we willing to do anything to avoid accepting it's over. we'll be a better, more attentive partner. Everything that's been wrong, we'll make right. The thought of being without your ex is so intolerable that you will make your own pain go away by winning him or her back, at any cost. Of course, you're not logical at this point (Love makes brain heavy, all of a sudden gravitation started working intensely on your brain it almost reaches from your knees to your heel).

We start with bargaining with ourselves first, we stand on the edge of what feels like an abyss, trying not to fall into the unknown. We cling to any hope we can, to prevent yourself from losing what we have come to depend on, for better or worse. However, during this phase, when we promise to fix all the problems between us, we are placing the entire burden of repairing, maintaining and sustaining a relationship onto ourselves. It's as if the responsibility is ours and ours alone to make it work this time. Try your hardest during this phase not to lose sight of the fact that both participants in the relationship contributed to its end. You can't possibly take responsibility for everything. Somewhere inside, you know that.

When we go through a difficult phase, we remember what people say about it forever.

It is hard to bargain with someone who is going through a tough time. When someone slides down from the peak, his sensitivity level tends to go up. He (or she) becomes so touchy & sensitive that at times other people wonder if he is, in fact, searching for an excuse to get hurt. In such a situation, one wrong, hard or unkind word can leave its impression like a footprint on a wet cement.

With rounds of clock, something will happen – he/she will understand that most of the people did not mean to hurt when they said 'that'...he/she will agree with their reasons to say it...he/she will acknowledge all the right things people (those who cares about you) said and did before & after 'that' thing... and eventually, he/she will even forgive everyone for what they had said.

However...bargaining can only briefly distract from the experience of loss. Reality inevitably comes crashing down, over and over again. Further, when you bargain, you are trying to take responsibility for why the relationship doesn't work, which may give you the illusion that you have control over it, perpetuating the belief that it's salvageable as long as you can just keep performing superhuman acts.

The Story Continues....

Shiv was leaning on his chair in his office, his phone resting in his hand, still reflecting the text he had sent to Shreya hours ago. He had convinced himself that this time, this message, would bring a breakthrough. But the silence in return was deafening.

The ache of rejection gnawed at him, sharper this time. His mind replayed their final moments together over and over again, like a broken record. "Why can't she just see how much I care? " He had already begged her once, explained his mistakes, promised he'd do better. The hope, like a fleeting drug, had made him believe that maybe, just maybe, he could fix everything. If only I can get her back. Maybe I can show her I'm worth it.

But why was it always like this? Why did they have to break up in the first place? His thoughts spiralled.

The pain was intolerable. The emptiness in his chest felt like it would never be filled. In this moment, Shiv realized something he hadn't allowed himself to admit before: This wasn't the first time he'd been through this cycle. He had tried and failed to win her back before. They had broken up, gotten back together, broken up again... It had all become a blur of endless apologies, promises, and efforts that never quite reached the heart of the issue.

"Mistakes are useless only if we don't learn from them," he muttered to himself, recalling something his friend had once told him. But was he really learning? Or was he just going through the motions, hoping for a different result?

Shiv stood up and paced around the cabin. His phone buzzed once more, but it wasn't Shreya. He glanced at it, his heart sinking. Even now, I'm waiting for a message that won't come.

He'd tried everything, it seemed. He'd promised to change, to listen more, to be better. He'd apologized endlessly for the things he didn't understand while they were together, yet the more he tried, the more distant she became. It wasn't because she was cruel; it was because she was cold. Detached. As if, somewhere in the last few months, she had sealed herself off from him entirely. She didn't shout, didn't curse him, didn't do anything that could have made him hate her but she had moved on in a way that he couldn't even comprehend.

And Shiv? He was still stuck, cycling through the same pattern of self-doubt and regret, as if each attempt at reconciliation was a desperate plea for the past to come alive again.
His phone screen blinked. A message from his best friend Mayank.

"Bro, how's it going? You still stuck on this?"

Shiv felt a wave of frustration. Why couldn't anyone understand? He quickly typed back, his fingers trembling.

"I don't get it, Mayank. She's not even trying to meet me halfway. I've done everything. I told her I'll change, I'll be better, but she just... she's gone. And now, I don't know if I can even handle this anymore."

Mayank's reply was swift: "Shiv, you're doing this again. You're holding on to something that isn't coming back. You can't keep chasing something that doesn't want to be caught."

Shiv felt a knot tighten in his stomach. "I know, I know," he replied. "But... it hurts too much. I just... can't stop thinking about her."

Mayank's response hit him harder than he expected: "You're in a loop, bro. You're hurting yourself more by holding on. And every time you go back, it's like you're reliving the same pain all over again. You're stuck in this relapse. The truth is, she's moved on. You need to move on, too."

The words stung, but deep down, Shiv knew he wasn't hearing anything new. Wasn't this the reality he had been avoiding? He had done this before promised change, given assurances, but the result was always the same. She was cold, distant, unreachable. And somewhere in the process, he had lost sight of himself, chasing a relationship that wasn't meant to be. Maybe I've become the same person I'm trying to fix.

He dropped his phone on the bed, the weight of Mayank's message sinking in. The pain of rejection is unbearable, yes. But is this pain worth it? He had to admit it: The answer was NO.

Shiv rubbed his face in frustration. I'm not going to beg her anymore. I can't keep doing this. He knew the pattern all too well. He had seen it before in other relationships and now in his own: the desperate cycle of relapse. Every time he tried to fix things, tried to bring back what was lost, it only led to more hurt.

It was hard. It was crushing. But somewhere inside him, he knew the truth: No amount of begging, no amount of promises, would bring her back. She was gone. And I needed to accept it.

His mind, weary from the struggle, tried to make sense of it all. Maybe I'll never understand why it happened, why she pulled away. But as he looked at the message from Mayank one more time, he whispered to himself, "Mujhe apni galtiyon ko samajhna hoga. Aur jo chala gaya, usse rakhna nahi."

The bitterness of the relapse still lingered, but the fog was starting to lift. I can't keep holding on to something that isn't coming back.

He stood up, walked to the window, and let the cool night air hit his face. Maybe, just maybe, it was time to let go. For his own peace. For his own growth.

The battle wasn't over. But for the first time, Shiv knew he needed to stop fighting for something that no longer existed. The thing that was existed is The Level Four of Break Up "Relapse Autopsy"

LEVEL FOUR

Relapse Autopsy

"Mistakes are useless only if don't learn from them."

The pain of break-up is so intolerable, that we may actually be able to convince our ex to try again (this may be the first ever experience for some of us or maybe a repetitive experience with the same partner or new one). We'll temporarily relieve the agony of rejection/withdrawal.

However, You will not be able to carry the baggage of breaking-up relationship solo, despite your best efforts, I'm sorry to say, it probably won't end well this time, either. Unfortunately, we may need to go through this process of breaking up and reconciling more than once before we're absolutely convinced it's time to move on. And there are some people in our lives who don't quite qualify as 'bad' – because they don't shout, use abusive language, plot against, talk behind the back, cheat, curse or for that matter, they don't even wish you any evil but just move on and left you with the baggage of break-up.

They are very 'difficult' – they are rigid, cold, distant, they get on to your nerves/brain, can overlook your presence, build stonewall in conversations by not cooperating, Stiff to change, maybe self-centred. And the more painful is that, in dealing with this type of people, you often risk becoming one of the same types and if you wish not to became one you must know your time to move-on.

The Story Continues....

The quiet hum of the late-night streets outside was broken by the deafening roar inside Shiv's mind. He was sitting in his car on the roadside under his building. He paced back and forth in his room, his fists clenched tight as his thoughts swirled in chaos. How could she do this? Why didn't she see what we had?

The breakup had sent him twirling, and while the previous levels had left him bewildered and sad, this one hit differently. This wasn't just about longing for Shreya anymore. It wasn't even just about the endless questions he had asked himself.

It was anger. Anger at her. Anger at himself. Anger at the world. It surged through him like an uncontrollable wildfire. "Why the hell does she have to be so cold?" The thought repeated itself, each time becoming more suffocating. Shiv had never been an angry person, not at all. But now, with everything building up inside, he felt his chest sinking with each breath. He wanted to scream, to throw things, to make it stop to make her realize how badly she had hurt him.

But instead, he stood there, staring out the car window, fighting with himself. The feeling of wanting to lash out, to shatter everything in sight, was overwhelming. His mind flashed to Shreya's face, the last time they had spoken her cold, distant eyes. She was done with me. That finality had hit him harder than he ever expected.

He reached for his phone, feeling the impulse to text her, to demand answers. To say something that would make her feel the fury he was feeling, but then his thumb hovered over the screen. What's the point? She's not going to care. Not anymore.

The anger wasn't just directed at her. It wasn't just about the hurt she caused him—it was about everything he couldn't control, everything that had twirled out of his hands. "What did I do wrong? Why didn't I see it sooner?" The anger morphed into something deeper now, a mix of frustration and self-loathing. I let her slip away. I wasn't good enough for her. She doesn't need me anymore.

The darkness of the street felt suffocating as he collapsed onto his seat, burying his face in his hands. He could feel it the anger boiling beneath the surface. But then, through the rage, came something else: fear. Fear of facing himself, of realizing that he had no one to blame but himself. Fear that maybe, just maybe, he wasn't capable of doing better, of being better.

In his head, the words of his favourite actress Eva Mendes echoed "I don't usually lose my temper, but if I get angry, it's true - I'm scared."
Shiv felt that fear. It wasn't just anger at the breakup. It wasn't just about Shreya moving on without him. It was the raw, terrifying reality that this relationship, this bond that he had invested so much in, was now gone. The fear of being alone. Of being lost. Of not being enough. That's what had driven him to this point, this volatile moment where his emotions were as scattered as the stars in the sky.

The anger became a mask for the fear, for the shame that had been festering inside him since the breakup. If I could just be angry, if I could just blame her, maybe it wouldn't hurt so much.

He straightened the seat, took his phone. But this time, there was no impulse to call her. No desire to reach out. Something inside him had shifted. A realization, perhaps. Anger will not heal this. Anger will not bring her back.

Suddenly, the words he had read earlier came back to him—"Anger is the root cause of all misfortunes. Anger is the reason for bondage with this world. Anger reduces righteousness, hence give up anger." Shiv closed his eyes, the quote echoing in his mind. Maybe it was time to let go of the anger, to stop feeding the fire.

He knew, deep down, that holding onto this anger wasn't helping him. It wasn't bringing him peace. In fact, it was doing the opposite. It was dragging him deeper into a hole he couldn't seem to escape. The truth was, as much as he wanted to destroy everything in his path, he knew this wasn't the way forward. He was only destroying himself.

With a deep sigh, Shiv threw his phone onto the bed, the impulse to retaliate fading with the realization that he wasn't truly angry with Shreya. He was angry at himself, at the helplessness he felt. He was angry because, deep down, he knew he had failed. I couldn't save us.

But that didn't mean it was the end for him. It didn't mean he couldn't heal. Slowly, as he sat in the dim light of the street, he began to understand something important. Anger wouldn't solve anything. It was time to face the pain, to let go of the rage, and to move forward.

The relief wasn't immediate. The anger still simmered just below the surface. But Shiv had taken the first step. He was ready to let go of the destructive grip that anger had on him. It was time to stop looking backward and start moving forward. And as the weight of that realization settled over him, he whispered to himself, “Maybe this is the beginning of letting go. Maybe I deserve more than to keep punishing myself.” It was The Level Five of Break Up "The chagrin"

LEVEL FIVE

The chagrin

The famous American actress Eva Mendes said it so well.

"I don't usually lose my temper, but if I get angry, it's true - I'm scared."

When we are not able to connect with the feeling of anger break-up plummets you into the unknown, which will inflame uncertain fear with surmise, and when fear increases it change into anger and bounces/bursts with a spring effect. We feel like destroying everything that comes in our way. Sometimes it is so strong that you may feel like destroying yourself too. But, when anger sets in, it helps us in letting go of some of our fear, at least for some time. Once you're able to access anger, the experience can be empowering and manage the dopamine rush because at the very least there are shades of remembering you also exist in this cosmos & matter too, of feeling justified in realizing that you deserve more from a relationship or at least you try to convince yourself with this thought.

Depending on our specific tolerance of anger, life, and family experiences, intellect as well as our bizarre breakup, our anger is mostly directed at our partner, the situation, ourselves or maybe everything else.

The shining part of this drama is that our anger, no matter where it's headed, is meant to entitle us with power, whether we choose to see it that way or not.

When anger becomes permeable to us, it can provide headship and create a sense of aliveness in the universe that's become closed-ended or remit by the loss. It can also remind you that you deserve more. Even anger at yourself, as paralysing and self-defeating as it may be, is still part of the grieving process. So be wise while showing your anger in break-up.

क्रोधो मूलमनर्थानां क्रोधः संसारबन्धनम्।
धर्मक्षयकरः क्रोधः तस्मात् क्रोधं वविर्जयेत्॥

Means "Anger is the root cause of all misfortunes. Anger is the reason for bondage with this world. Anger reduces righteousness, hence give up anger."

The Story Continues....

Shiv stood by the window, Feeling the cool breeze brushing against his face as the world outside seemed to move in a rhythm he no longer quite understood. The months following his breakup with Shreya had been a blur of emotional chaos anger, sorrow, self-doubt, and a seemingly endless cycle of trying to piece himself back together. But now, something had changed. Shiv dialed Mayank on the phone...

"Kaha hai be tu...Sale break up se me deal kar raha hu or gayab tu ho agya hai..."

Mayank spoke in surprised voice- "Who is it...and how you got Shiv's mobile...where is he.."

Shiv.." Ha Ha Ha very funny... I am Shiv" Mayank- "Koi naya peddler mila hai kya seems you good really good stuff...kya hua bhai tujhe randi rona band kaise aaj and what is this spark in your voice"

After so many days Shiv had a long talk with Mayank...Shiv realized at least for the moment that it wasn't something that could be pinned down with words or neatly defined in a moment of clarity. It was more of a shift, a subtle feeling that came over him in fleeting bursts. Shiv would catch himself in the mirror and notice the way his eyes no longer seemed so hollow. A thought would cross his mind and instead of feeling the sharp sting of loss, it felt like an old wound that was healing, even if it wasn't fully closed.

"I'm not the same anymore," he thought to himself. It wasn't sadness anymore, not the kind that paralysed him in the early days after the breakup. It wasn't anger either. There was something new, something that felt like an opening to a different version of himself, a version that existed beyond the relationship that had once defined him.

The words of the old saying echoed in his mind "Time and tide wait for none." Time, the great healer, had worked its subtle magic, though it didn't always feel like it. There were moments when he felt strong and focused, a sense of control returning to his life. But then, there were moments when he felt weak and vulnerable, like the old wounds were fresh again, and it was a constant oscillation between strength and fragility.

"The wounds are still there... they may be dry, but as wet as the ocean inside." The pain wasn't gone. It wasn't that he had forgotten it; he hadn't forgotten Shreya or the love they had shared. But he had begun to understand something far deeper. The pain, the loss—it was part of the journey, but it didn't define him.

His phone buzzed, and for a moment, he wondered if it was Shreya. But then, he realized it didn't matter anymore. The thought didn't send him coiling like it once would have. Instead, he reached for it, glanced at the screen, and put it back down, a quiet acceptance settling over him.

He was different now. Not because he had fixed everything far from it but because he had begun to accept that healing wasn't a destination. It was a journey. And sometimes, healing didn't look the way we expected it to. It didn't come with clear answers or neatly wrapped closure. It came in small, almost imperceptible steps forward. And in those moments of clarity, Shiv realized that he wasn't just moving on. He was awakening.

It wasn't about Shreya anymore. It wasn't about her love or their failed relationship. It was about him. About rediscovering his own worth, his own identity. The relentless search for answers, the fixation on what went wrong—those things no longer held the power they once had over him. He was starting to see that love wasn't just about seeking it from others. The love he needed to focus on, to nourish, was the one he had for himself.

"Self-love," he murmured softly. It was the most difficult concept to grasp when your heart had been shattered, but it was also the most important. Self-love wasn't about vanity or selfishness. It was about recognizing your own value, understanding that you were worthy of love not because of what you did for others, not because of the approval you sought from external sources—but simply because you existed.

For the first time in months, Shiv felt a quiet but certain sense of peace settle within him. He was still healing. There were still days when the pain of the breakup would come crashing back, but now he knew it was part of the process. He didn't need to rush it. He didn't need to fix it. All he had to do was let it be.

The healing wasn't linear and it has its ups and downs sometimes, those ups and downs could be overwhelming. But he had learned to embrace them. To not run from the pain, but to let it wash over him and recede, just like the tide. It wasn't about being perfect or even "getting over" Shreya completely it was about learning to live fully with who he was becoming. To honour his growth, his mistakes, and his lessons.

Shiv took a deep breath, feeling the weight of the past months slowly lifting from his shoulders. The journey was far from over, but he was no longer lost in the dark. He had awakened to something deeper within himself. And in that moment, for the first time in a long while, he felt alive in a way that wasn't dependent on anyone else. It was the beginning of something new, something real. The awakening had begun. Shiv closed his eyes, whispering to himself, "I am enough. I am worthy." The road ahead was unknown, but he was ready to walk it. He was ready to meet himself again this time, not through anyone else's eyes, but through his own. Welcome to Level Six "The Awakening".

LEVEL SIX

The Awakening

As the saying the saying goes...time and tide wait for none, you begin to feel a shift inside. It id very subtle at first like a whisper in the background in an arena, but it's there. You have on-and-off thoughts or encounters where you realise you're not the same person you were before, A part of you is missing....it has been taken away or gone with that person.

If you have these thoughts then welcome to level six...I name it "The Awakening". Level six is the first foot towards a new journey...A journey from Buddu to Buddha or Gargi.

यह समय है जब इस सदि्धार्थ को नकिलना चाहिए इस मझधार से ...जसिका कोई कनिारा नहीं है ...इस सदि्धार्थ को नकिलना चाहिए बुद्ध होने को ...कनि्तु ये रात यशोधरा बनकर सदि्धार्थ को रोकेगी ....बुद्ध होने से...और सदि्धार्थ रुका तो वो न सदि्धार्थ रहेगा ...न यशोधरा ...वो आधा बुद्धा पौने सदि्धार्थ और वाकी यशोधरा हो कर रह जायेगा..

You start to elevate yourself to see things from a higher level....but wait....hold your horse...if you are expecting your Immunoglobulins have already started to act. Healing is started then "हुनूज़ दलि्ली दूर अस्त"... means the wounds are still there.. they may be a little dry but as wet as the ocean inside...the healing is nowhere close. The strength that emerges in you fades away in fractions of seconds and you get weak every 30 seconds. This oscillation from rock-hard to butter-soft continues for a pretty good time. However, every breakup is an opportunity for growth, and though it feels impossible in the beginning, you soon realize that you have awakened to a new sense of self.

The wounds are still there, but they're a bit dry. You start to rediscover who you are outside of the relationship, and for the first time in a long while, you focus entirely on yourself.

The pain of the breakup begins to fade, not because it didn't matter, but because you've learned from it. You've stopped trying to find the "why" in the other person's actions or the meaning in the words they left behind. Instead, you've focused on understanding why you felt the way you did, what you were seeking in the relationship, and how you can move forward in a way that honours who you are.

During this phase, the things that may help you to engage with hobbies, reconnect with friends or explore new things you'd forgotten about. You start to see that there's more to life than the relationship that once consumed you. And it's not that you've forgotten; it's that you've forgiven not just the other person, but yourself. Forgiveness is not a one-time event. It's an ongoing process, a conscious choice to free yourself from the past. The real awakening happens when you realize that while love is vital, it should never define your worth. Self-love is the most important love to nurture...In our search for love, we often look outward towards other people, situations, or external factors to fill a void within us. We believe that being loved by someone else will heal our wounds, make us feel complete, or give our lives meaning. This external validation, while gratifying in the moment, can be temporary. It's easy to fall into the trap of seeking love from others to fill an emotional deficit one that can only be healed by developing a strong, unconditional love for yourself. True and lasting love starts from within.

Falling in love with yourself is not about narcissism or selfishness; it's about cultivating a deep sense of self-acceptance, self-compassion, and self-worth. It's about recognizing that you are deserving of love, not because of what you do or how you make others feel, but simply because you exist. This is the foundation on which a healthy, thriving relationship with another person can be built and realization and acceptance level is what I call "The Awakening"

The Story Continues....

Shiv sat in the quiet on his recliner in his room looking at the panoramic view of the city lights, it felt like spilling through the window like an ocean of stars stretching to the horizon. It had been a while since he'd last truly felt at peace. For weeks, the pain had been an unrelenting companion, pulling him through the motions of life, each day feeling like he was wading through a thick fog. But tonight, it felt different. There was a stillness, a calmness that had gently settled within him, like the calm after a storm.

He leaned back in his chair, closing his eyes, the memories of Shreya flooding his mind. It was as though he could still feel her presence, She was in his muscle memories, the laughter they once shared, the quiet moments, the late-night talks, the road trips. They had been happy real happiness, at least for a time. But happiness, like everything else in life, had a shelf life. And now, the past seemed like an echo, soft and distant, but no less important.

For the first time, Shiv wasn't angry. He wasn't upset or torn between wanting to turn back time. Instead, he felt... quiet. At peace with what had been, and even more so, with what had ended.

It was a realization that came gently, like a whisper, barely audible at first, but slowly growing in significance. Acceptance. The kind of acceptance that comes not from resignation, but from understanding that sometimes, things are meant to be the way they are. Some relationships are never meant to last forever. And that doesn't make them any less real, any less meaningful.

Shiv was reading a poem "I am Learning" which Mayank shared with him. Shiv usually don't like to read fiction or poetry but since this was shared by Mayank he gave it a thought...it was written by some new comer writer **Lokesh Vishwakarma** and goes like-

"I am learning gradually that, I should not react to every single thing that bothers me,
I am learning by degrees that, I should not hurt those who had hurt me.
I am learning inch-by-inch that perhaps the biggest sense of reasoning is to move away rather than get into it.
I am learning drop-by-drop that, the energy that I spend in reacting to every bad behaviour that accompanies me empties and prevents me from seeing other good things.
I am learning in piecemeal that, I will not get from people the treatment that I expect.
I am learning in inchmeal that, Its very costly and time-consuming process to win someone's heart & I can't make everyone happy in the cosmos. If I do so I'll get filled by the emptiness in the end.
I am learning serenely that, Sometimes its better to no reply & it doesn't mean it is acceptable to me, But rather I think it is better to rise above so I can be huge.
I am learning unassumingly that, Sometimes silence speaks louder than words.
I am learning placidly that, I must not give privilege to anyone to overrule my feelings, emotions & Thoughts.
I am learning patiently that, My reaction will not change anything, neither it will change people around me magically.
I am learning meekly that, entire universe become so beautiful when we focus on our inner world than focusing on the events around us.
I am learning calmly that, life is a wisecrack to laugh on, it's not a tragedy to morn on.
I learnt affably that, I can't control the whole cosmos; I have to start accepting life, things, people as they are.

I learnt enlighteningly that, I need to work for myself and my inner peace and I have realized that giving 'NO' reaction to every little thing that worries is the 'first element' of an enlightened, healthy and happy life."

This poem went right into his head he got the zest of it "We cannot change anything until we accept it," It struck him deeply now. Acceptance wasn't giving up. It wasn't about throwing in the towel and saying, "I'm done." No, it was the quiet surrender to the fact that things unfolded the way they were meant to. The relationship had taught him something valuable something he could carry with him, not as a wound, but as a lesson. A lesson that sometimes, people come into our lives for a reason, to teach us, to challenge us, and then to let us go.

Shiv could feel the weight lifting. He no longer carried the burden of blame, of second-guessing every decision he'd made, every word he'd spoken. What was meant to be, was. And for that, he was grateful. Not because it was easy, but because it had been real.

He let out a breath he hadn't realized he was holding. There was no more wondering if he could have done something differently, no more wishing the story could have had a different ending. It had ended, and in that ending, there was a quiet peace. A peace that spoke to him of new beginnings, of self-love, of understanding that he was whole without Shreya, without anyone.

It wasn't that he had forgotten her; he hadn't. She had been part of his life, part of his growth. And that mattered. The love they had shared was real, and it would always have a place in his heart. But now, Shiv understood that love, true love was not about being with someone else. It was about being with yourself first. It was about finding peace within, about knowing that you were enough as you were, without needing anyone to fill the empty spaces.

The past had left its scars, yes, but those scars had healed. Slowly, tenderly, over time. They had turned into something else a mark of who he was, who he had become. And they no longer defined him.

Shiv was in deep thoughts and suddenly his phone shook... it was another text from Mayank..."Love is like a fart... if you have to force it, it's probably shit." ....Shiv smiled at the ridiculousness after reading this...

Mayank send another text..." I though poem padke jyda senty naa ho jaye so to lighten up the mood I texted this...hope tere sade thobde per thodi smile aayi hogi..."

It was very lame but Shiv thought there was truth in it. Love shouldn't be forced. When it's meant to be, it flows effortlessly. And when it's not, it's okay to let it go. Forcing something that is no longer right would only prolong the suffering. And Shiv had learned that lesson the hard way.

His phone buzzed on the table, snapping him back to the present. He glanced at it for a moment but didn't reach for it. He didn't need to anymore. The validation, the approval, the constant need for someone else to make him feel complete he no longer sought it. Not from her, not from anyone. He was whole.
The changing seasons of life, the fleeting moments of joy and sorrow, the inevitable ebb and flow of emotions they were all temporary. They would come, and they would go. And in that constant change, Shiv had learned to tolerate without being disturbed. He had learned to let go without regret. To live without holding on to the past.

He sat for a while longer, letting the city lights flicker softly outside, his heart lighter than it had been in months. There was no need to force anything. The story was already written. It wasn't always the way he wanted it to be, but it had been enough. And now, with every fibber of his being, he could say it: he was ready to move forward. Not because he had to, but because he had found peace in his acceptance.

He wasn't waiting for someone else to complete him. He had finally accepted that he was enough—just as he was. And that, in itself, was the greatest kind of love he could offer: love for himself. He had learned to hold himself, to cherish himself, and that was all he needed for now.

The journey wasn't over. But Shiv was no longer afraid of it. The path ahead was his to walk, full of new beginnings, new possibilities, and a love that was pure and self-sustained. He had learned the hard way, but he had learned. And with that, he stepped forward, ready for the next chapter of his life. The Level Seven went little smoothly for Shiv and left the following learnings

LEVEL SEVEN

The Acceptance

"We cannot change anything until we accept it. Condemnation does not liberate, it oppresses."

— Carl Jung

The 7th level...you come to the bittersweet realization that not all relationships are meant to last forever, and that's okay. This phase comes after the initial shock, anger, and heartache. It is the moment when you awaken to the truth that some relationships are not destined to continue, not because they were failures or either of you has given your best to make it work but because they were never meant to be permanent. These relationships enter our lives to shape our character and prepare us for a love that is better aligned with the person we have become.

Acceptance here is not a form of resignation it is a state of peace...after the long hustle and noise of echoing beeps, it's finally the calming silence that feels so soothing to your ears. It's the realization that, while we may long for things to have turned out differently, they couldn't have. What was meant to be, was. And that in itself is enough. This acceptance is about letting go of the narrative that something "should" have been different and embracing the understanding that the relationship, however painful its end, was an important part of our journey.

When we begin to understand that not every person we meet is meant to stay in our life forever. The people we encounter in our lives come with their own journeys, paths that may be completely different from ours. Even though we may have shared deep love and meaningful moments, the paths we take might diverge at some point. That's the essence of acceptance: understanding that some people are simply not the right match for us, no matter how much we may have wanted it to be different.

Trying to force a relationship to continue when it is clear that it has come to an end only prolongs the suffering. It's a very lame reference but I read somewhere that love is like a fart... if you have to force it's probably shit.

We cannot change the trajectory of someone else's life or make them stay when it's no longer right. In accepting this reality, we release the need to fight against it, and we allow ourselves to heal. We begin to honour the end of the relationship as a natural part of the cycle, not something to be resisted. With this acceptance, we free ourselves from the chains of regret and heartache, and we regain the dignity and grace to move forward.

You also begin to understand that love is not just about being with someone it's about being with yourself first. It's only when you are content and whole on your own that you can truly be open to love again, in a way that's healthy and fulfilling.

This stage is about letting go of the idea that you could have done something differently to prevent the breakup. The truth is, that we all play our parts in relationships, but some things are simply out of our control. The more you accept that the relationship ended because it was meant to, the sooner you will find peace.

In this space, you stop blaming yourself or the other person. You stop trying to rewrite the past and instead, choose to focus on the lessons learned, the growth that has occurred, and the wisdom that comes from experiencing such an intimate connection. There is a quiet understanding that as painful as it may be, this ending was an essential step toward becoming who you are meant to be.

A key realization that comes with acceptance is the understanding that love is not just about being with someone else; it's about being with yourself first. The pain of a breakup often arises from the fear of being alone, of feeling incomplete without someone to share our lives with. But true healing happens when we embrace solitude, when we find fulfillment within ourselves, and when we recognize that we are whole on our own.

During this phase of acceptance, you come to understand that you are worthy of love, not because someone else affirms it, but because you affirm it for yourself. Only when you are content and whole within yourself can you truly be open to love again in a way that is healthy, balanced, and fulfilling. This is the essence of self-love the realization that you are enough, just as you are, without needing someone else to complete you.

As you move through this phase, you start to nurture yourself, rediscover your passions, and prioritize your own well-being. You embrace the idea that your happiness is not dependent on being in a relationship. This self-acceptance lays the foundation for a stronger, more resilient version of yourself, one that is ready for a love that is built on mutual respect, understanding, and true connection.

As Krishna explains in chapter 2, Verse 14 in Shree Mad Bhagwat Geeta

मात्रास्पर्शास्तु कौन्तेय शीतोष्णसुखदुःखदाः ।
आगमापायिनोऽनित्यास्तांस्तितिक्षस्व भारत ॥

This means the non-permanent appearance of happiness and distress, and their disappearance in due course, are like the appearance and disappearance of winter and summer seasons. They arise from sense perception and one must learn to tolerate them without being disturbed.

The Story Continues....

Months had passed, and Shiv felt the weight of the past slowly lift. Now all Shiv has is the beautiful memories of their time together. He again started to smile remembering of Shreya. What once seemed like an endless, raw wound had now softened into a place of peace. He had walked through the darkness, and now, he was beginning to see the light. The pain of the breakup had shaped him in ways he never imagined. His heart, once shattered, was now healed, not by time alone, but by understanding.

Through the hurt, Shiv had learned that love begins within. It is not about searching for someone to complete us, but about recognizing the wholeness we already carry. The scars that once marked him were now symbols of his strength, his resilience, and his growth. The journey through heartache had taught him that true transformation is not instant; it's a slow unfolding of the self.

Shiv now understood that love, in its truest form, enhances rather than diminishes us. He was no longer searching for someone to fill the emptiness he once felt. The emptiness had never existed it was a misconception, a belief. He was whole, just as he was.

As he moved forward, Shiv realized that the pain of heartbreak had unlocked a hidden power within him, a creative force he never knew existed. The power of love and heartbreak had transformed his suffering into strength, his loss into growth.

He no longer lived in regret. He had learned to embrace the lessons of the past, to find meaning in every experience. He was free—free from the need to control, to possess, to cling. His transformation was complete. And in this newfound freedom, Shiv knew that he was finally ready to love not because he needed someone to complete him, but because he was already whole.

This, he realized, was only the beginning and here we reached to the Final Level of Break up "

LEVEL EIGHT

The Transformation

"Transformation is a process, and as life happens there are tons of ups and downs. It's a journey of discovery – there are moments on mountaintops and moments in deep valleys of despair."

— Rick Warren

Now, time moves, and you also start to move in your life with acceptance. You start to transform for the better, which is much needed. The ugly and creepy-looking larva turns into an eye-catching, beautiful butterfly by transformation. Transformation can bring the magic back in your life.

Months have passed since the breakup, and you look back with clarity. The rawness of the pain you once felt has begun to fade, replaced by a deeper understanding of the journey you've walked. Initially, you may have been consumed with thoughts of "what could have been" imagining alternate realities where the relationship stayed intact. But now, you've found a sense of peace in the present moment. The memories, once so intense, have been transformed into something more serene—a memory that, though marked by its share of sorrow, also carries with it deep gratitude. You no longer see the past through the lens of regret, but as a chapter that played a crucial role in shaping who you are today.

At this level of breakup, your wounds finally start to dry inside-out, the phase of healing is marked by a sense of acceptance. The emotional scars that once seemed so deep have become the very things that have allowed you to grow. You've come to realize that each heartache, each moment of difficulty, was part of a larger plan, one that was not about the other person, but about you and your own evolution. You may have heard it before, but now you know it to be true: *What doesn't kill you makes you stronger.* Through the pain, you have learned resilience, patience, and self-compassion. You've embraced the truth that life's challenges are not roadblocks but stepping stones, guiding you toward a deeper understanding of yourself.

You've become a stronger, more resilient version of yourself. You can relate more to the story of Meraki which goes like-

"God has given great power to man after he created him, and Man, being a man was not able to handle that limitless power. He had an illusion that he is God himself, He was proud of that supreme power he had, he became egoistic, cruel and rude to other animals. So God decided to take back that power and he asked his angels to hide it somewhere so man could hardly find it.

1st Angel suggested hiding it deep down in the ground, the God said no man will find & dig it out, as they dug diamonds.

2nd Angel said sink it deep into the ocean, God replied Man will find that out as well like they found pearls.

3rd Angel advised putting it at the peak of a mountain, God said the man would climb that too as they climbed the Himalayas.

So after so much brainstorming, finally, they reach a conclusion to hide it in man's heart, so he could not find it out easily & the key to this limitless power is only two Love & heartbreak (Breakup).

Now the dopamine rush/adrenaline rush has access to that limitless power. There are only two ways to get it, 1st love but the misery is that we use all our emotional power of creation & it does create magic in poetry, literature, painting, science, philosophy, entrepreneurship, cooking or any other field of creation. Greek used to call it Miraki (the power of doing great things with the energy of love/heartbreak). This is why the food cooked by our mom has a different taste in it, & the funny part is I believe my mother is the best cook in the world and my wife is a pathetic cook. ironically my father thinks the same.

Anyway, the point is the energy of love can make a simple food taste great. So the energy of love has that x-factor in it, to make simple things great. But there is a great loophole also in love, When we are in love we do great or impossible things for your love. all our power is limited to one person, we don't even think about anyone else or ourselves. As a human being, we have the ability to transfer our emotional energy, and if we do that, we can enable our immense potential to do great things i.g. Farhad did for Shirin he flowed a milk river for her.

Now heartbreak, you might have heard one Hindi proverb "घायल शेर ज़्यादा खरतनाक होता हैं". So the Miraki of heartbreak/ break up is 100 times more powerful than the Miraki of love. A heartbreak can happen by 3 means only, the partner said NO, Cheated on You or died. I went down to nerve lane inside my mind to find the answer of it. when I had a heartbreak.

The final level is about realizing the Meraki... understanding that we are the creators of our happiness. We begin to make choices that are in alignment with our values and our newfound understanding of what love truly is. The baggage of the past is no longer weighing us down, and we begin to move through life with a renewed sense of purpose and direction.

If love enters your life again, we're no longer searching for someone to "complete" us. We are already whole. Instead, we seek someone who complements the life we've built for ourselves—a partner who adds joy, not a sense of neediness. There a Sanskrit saying न मुमुक्षुं प्रयितमा *means do not hold on to what is dear if it hinders growth,* reminds us that love is not about holding on for fear of loss; it is about letting go when it no longer serves the higher good. Letting go does not mean giving up; it means trusting that you are both better off moving forward separately.

Transformation is not a sudden shift, but rather a slow unfolding process. The pieces of your life, once fragmented, are coming together in a way that feels more authentic. We start to recognize that the relationships and experiences we have had though sometimes painful were precisely what we needed to become the person we are today. We now look back on the past and, instead of asking "Why did this happen?", we begin to ask, "What can we learn from this?" This shift in perspective changes everything. We no longer live in regret; instead, we live in gratitude. We carry the lessons from the past with us but are no longer burdened by the weight of old wounds.
One of the most liberating realizations in this phase is that love is not something you need to search for. Love, in its truest form, begins with loving yourself first. In the past, perhaps you were

searching for someone to complete you, to fill a space within you that you thought was empty. But now, you realize that this emptiness was never real. You were always whole and now you found yourself this स्वयमप्राप्ति *Self-realization or self-fulfillment* reminds us that fulfillment comes from within. True love is not about searching for someone to complete you; it is about sharing your already complete self with another. This understanding opens you up to a deeper and more fulfilling kind of love, one that is based on mutual growth, respect, and shared happiness. You begin to seek a partner not out of need, but out of desire to add more joy and beauty to the life you've already cultivated. You are not looking for someone to save you or make you whole. Instead, you seek someone who complements you, someone who adds light to the life you are already building.

विमुक्ति में प्रेम है, स्वातंत्र्य में खुशी है...**is** echoes within your heart. You now understand that love should never be a prison but rather an expansive force that allows both individuals to grow and thrive. True love is not about holding on tightly or clinging to someone for fear of being alone; it is about letting go of the need to control, to possess, and allowing both people to live freely, to love freely. You understand that love, in its highest form, does not diminish you; it enhances you. This transformation from incomplete to complete completes you as a human. You are now

निष्कलंकं, निर्विकारं

मनः एव मनुष्याणां कारणं बन्ध-मोक्षयोः।

The mind alone is the cause of bondage and liberation for humans.

THINGS TO REMEMBER IN A RELATIONSHIP

"Love is forever, if not then it's not Love..."

"Being deeply **loved** by someone gives you strength, while **loving** someone deeply gives you courage." – Lao Tzu
It's almost impossible to find a 'low maintenance...no melodramatic...less fluctuating.... stable... and a loyal partner who is still loving. it is a rare privilege to have in the contemporary era.

In the contemporary world, most relationships are a result of either a sentimental movie, Netflix web-series or a musically/Tik-Tok video'.

These days, You can see two major patterns in relationships – First, partners are so obsessed with each other that they are completely occupying to suffocating level to each other by being together all the time or intertwining their lives needlessly.

As an outcome, it hurts our partner and we expect that a 'sorry' should mend it immediately. and the irony is our 'sorry' didn't even come out of guilt that you must feel but it is an introspection you did at your own pace.

Now the second type, partners are connected so superficially as if they have a trial version of some app, or hacked an app, keep using it but keep clicking on 'Later' when there is a question about registering.

This is the biggest irony in the modern times on the green earth of God, Polar opposites are contemporary to each other. But the true love I believes still exist in a few rare lucky relationships, in which, both partners know that yes, it is there......the LOVE.......to anchor someone without cutting their wing.

Moreover, in the second type of relationship, it is "lust" covered with the skin of love, so beware of your type of relationship.

"Toxicity of EVERYTHING"

"अग्निशेषमृणशेषं शत्रुशेषं तथैव च |
पुनः पुनः प्रवर्धेत तस्माच्छेषं न कारयेत् ||"

"If a fire, a loan, or an enemy(Desire) continues to exist even to a small extent, it will grow again and again; so do not let anyone of it continue to exist even to a small extent."

All of us have been involved in a relationship either with persons or things at one time or another in our lifetimes which are TOXIC in nature.

The toxicity level of these may vary from person to person or from thing to thing. Some people/things behave as slow poison it takes too much time to recognize their harm & they are addictive too. It will take more time to come out from this addiction of things/people.

Toxicity comes in various forms like the desire, comfort, need, a thrust, trust & so on. Toxicity of relationships or things can damage and leave long-lasting effects on individuals brain, mind, heart & soul. So be aware of your relations and addictions whether it is a personal relationship involving a family member, lover or a friend, or a professional relationship involving a co-worker or a boss or a routine of your life.
Entering into a toxic relationship with person or thing can result in severe inner conflict that can potentially lead to anger, depression or anxiety. It is important to recognize the red flags associated with toxic individuals and toxic relationships, in order to prevent any unnecessary emotional and mental turmoil.

"If a fire, a loan, or an enemy (Desire) continues to exist even to a small extent, it will grow again and again,,,,,,,,

So kill it at its 1st identification,,,,, because if something is giving you even a pinch of mental or emotional pressure it's a TOXIC relation.

"Adjust but must ADD JUSTice to yourself..."

In life, everyone has to adjust or compromise in some or other way. there are times when we do so because there is something we want to hold back or procure, preserve or save whether – a relationship...an association... a person......a thought.......or an arrangement which gives us comfort or meaning of being us.

So, at our best, with our best efforts, we adjust, for one or two times and unconsciously we enter into a never-ending loop of compromises and adjustments. We adjust more and more – to avoid confrontation to 'not hurt someone', to let it pass to 'not create a scene' to maintain dignity, to give another chance, to respect what is at stake, or probably to avoid exploding and letting out your own worse side, to save a beauty of being human, beauty of being in relation (As a friend, colleague or boy/girlfriend).

This goes on, and without even giving it a thought you lost yourself, You merely became a public pot. then one day, we look at yourself and go absolutely numb... we can't recognize the person in the mirror, we just become a shadow of our own compromises... you can't even recall who you originally were... what was it like to be you... who were you really at the core. That day, a realization dawn upon you...
...that you have adjusted successfully to save 'that something'...
...but have ended up losing something more important –that is You.

So, don't try to be a cup of tea for everyone, If you do so surely you will end up being a spitting pot for everyone.

Nothing wrong with adjustments and compromises the only err in it is, you must know the bottom line of the same, You must know when to adjust and how much to adjust or where to stop.

Don't compromise or adjust beyond your limits,

How you treat other in your shiny days and how you treat yourself in your cloudy days. will make you what kind of person you are.

So always treat yourself with best what you can afford.

“Let's Fall in LOVE & Rise in LIFE....”

"Love has nothing to do with what you are expecting to get, it's what you are expected to give - which is everything, it is about falling not rising, losing not gaining, giving not taking."

Relationships are continually moving between times, we experience the warmth of the shining Sun of "Perfect Love" in the unclouded sky; shining brightly and the times of dark cloudy sky, which covers this blissfulness of Sun of love by the negative thoughts of our human misery.

But we must remember this, as the universe is infinite & the clouds could -not cover the Sun always, So in our relationships that if we move intelligently then we can easily cross the times when the clouds of our ego, lust, dubiety, envy, misunderstanding, superiority complex etc. covers the bask of our love, just remember that its a mortal phenomenon & love is Shaswat (immortal), So blissful that it shines through the Soul of each person in this world. Each human being is Divine in nature at the Soul level. So just ignore the negative traits or temporary clouds of a person & Love that person unconditionally; fall in love don't try to rise in love, just give and that's define everything.

And when we fall in love with someone, we love to be in the company of that person, every single wise or silly act of that person increase your feelings towards him or her. As the bright, warm sunrays of love come gushing through that person's Soul & we feel blissful, we feel complete, Love has great power of creation & it is beyond the qualities of ours like ego, mistrust, hatred, envy, anger etc. But with our limited consciousness, we try to understand the infinite phenomena of love and we lead to having the problems in our relations. The same person who seemed so lovable once becomes an object of hatred because we tried to rise in love.

"What we need to learn in life is how to Love people and use things, instead of using people and Loving things."

As Mother Terasa said, "There is more hunger for Love and Appreciation in this world than for bread."

So, let's Fall In LOVE, instead of rising in LOVE.....

AN APOLOGY TO MYSELF

Dear me, I would like to apologize to you for letting you settle less than you deserve.
Dear me, I have penitence for not taking the less traveled road into yellow woods and going with "Masses", even after knowing most of the time the "M" is missing.
Dear me, I remorse for chasing fireflies when I know you deserve the sun. I am in contrition for accepting the waves and not waiting for the ocean.
Dear me, I am sorry for giving too much importance to people for whom you may not even have existed, this poem is my statement of mea culpa & I took full responsibility for making you feel less important and putting questions on your existence and making you feel pity.
Dear me, I have great regret for making you fall for the wrong people, the wrong things at the wrong time. I am sorry for every time I have turned a deaf ear and not heard your inner voice, most of the time you were whispering, and I would have listened to you.
Dear me, I redress for not noticing actions and just buying the words from people, even when there was a great discrepancy in their words and actions, sometimes their words were so harsh on you, that is has broke you into parts.
Dear me, I write this poem with a heavy heart, but I hope it brings you peace and comfort. I am deeply sorry for any pain or suffering I have caused you, and I promise to do better in the future. You are my everything, and I will always be here for you.

FINAL THOUGHT

Finally, love is a journey of growth, learning, and healing and breakups are undeniably painful, but they are also powerful opportunities for transformation. We need to understand and make sure this transformation must not be just an ecdysiast where you just shed your outer layer but must be a complete metamorphosis so when you go through this transformation you come out from your cocoon as a butterfly with lots of colours and new wings...red bull may not give you wings literally but love can and it should.

Through this metamorphosis, we are reshaped, realigned, and reconnected with who we are meant to be. It's okay to feel lost, to grieve, and to question what went wrong. But remember that every experience, every heartbreak, every loss, is preparing you for something greater. You are worthy of love, and it begins with loving yourself first.

As you rise from the ashes of your past relationship, you will find that the world is full of new possibilities, new connections, and new chances for happiness. Love may come again, but this time, it will be different because you will be different. And that's the most beautiful transformation of all.

The main irony of relationship end, is when an epic relationship ends particularly one that was so intense and all-consuming the aftermath can often feel like an unpredictable emotional storm. this is as uproarious as it was we may think we've moved on, that we've navigated the worst of it, only to be blindsided by a sudden surge of confusion, anger, or overwhelming sadness.

This emotional upheaval might seem out of nowhere, and it's common to feel as though we're back at square one.
The truth is, the more chaotic and tumultuous the relationship was, the more chaotic your emotional response will likely be in its wake. But why is this? Why do the echoes of the past resurface so strongly, sometimes long after you thought you had healed?

In an uproarious relationship, a relationship filled with constant fighting, resentment, jealousy, insecurity, blaming, encroaching the personal boundaries and emotional rollercoasters, the brain becomes overstimulated. Our nervous system gets used to a high level of intensity, whether from arguments, emotional highs, or a constant state of anxiety. In such a relationship, even moments of calm can feel temporary or fleeting. The fight-or-flight response becomes a part of our everyday experience.

When the relationship ends, there is a sudden, jarring drop in this constant stimulation. For a while, we may feel a sense of relief, or even peace, as the chaos subsides. However, as time passes, we may unexpectedly find ourselves overwhelmed by emotions that seem to come out of nowhere. The mind, no longer accustomed to the tension and stimulation of the past relationship, now has to cope with the sudden stillness, which can feel eerily uncomfortable.

It's like an addict who has been accustomed to a constant rush when that rush disappears, it leaves behind a sense of emptiness, even confusion. This emotional emptiness can feel overwhelming and even alienating, as our brain adjusts to a new, calmer reality.

One of the most jarring aspects of post-breakup emotions is how they can swing unpredictably from one extreme to another. You might feel utterly lost, as if you're shrinking into nothingness, only to be hit with waves of intense rage or shame. This emotional back-and-forth can feel exhausting and destabilizing, especially when you struggle to understand why you feel so disconnected from yourself.

The experience of emotional whiplash feeling both numb and enraged at the same time can be especially disorienting. It's as if our body and mind are at war with each other, pulling us in opposite directions. This emotional turbulence is often a sign of deep-seated trauma from the relationship that was never properly processed. While we were in the relationship, we were constantly in survival mode, managing the chaos and doing our best to hold things together. Now, after the relationship has ended, the floodgates of unresolved trauma have opened.

An "uproarious" relationship is far more than just a series of constant arguments or misunderstandings or no understanding at all.. we both gradually become poles apart like a day and night never agreeing on one thing or thought. It is a dynamic shaped by manipulation, emotional cruelty, unpredictability, and an overwhelming sense of emotional instability or insecurity where both persons feel they are culprits, both are prey and predators. The emotional landscape is fraught with tension, where each moment feels like walking on a tightrope, unsure of what might trigger the next upheaval. How the person will react, it may go from your my everything to you are nothing in seconds.

This kind of relationship often carries elements of emotional abuse, where subtle or overt forms of control, degradation, and invalidation can leave lasting scars; scars that are not always visible, even to yourself. These emotional wounds might go unnoticed at first, especially when you are caught up in the intensity of the connection, or when the emotional highs of the relationship temporarily drown out the deeper issues.

In such a relationship, intense emotions, whether passionate love or explosive anger, become both a survival mechanism and a destructive force. The chaos, while painful, offers a strange sense of familiarity and even comfort. It becomes the only way to feel alive, to feel something—anything in a relationship that is emotionally perilous. Our brain, constantly on high alert, operates in a state of heightened awareness, adapting to and reacting to every external trigger, every word, and every action. It becomes exhausting to exist in this constant state of emotional turbulence, where the need to survive, to protect ourselves, often overshadows our ability to recognize the damage being done.

The emotional volatility serves as a backdrop to our daily existence, compelling us to react in ways that feel instinctive, but ultimately lead to further conflict and confusion. We may have been so immersed in the cycle of highs and lows that we didn't fully realize the toll it was taking on our mental and emotional well-being. The unpredictability becomes a cruel substitute for stability, and it's only in the aftermath when the relationship ends that the true weight of this emotional turmoil comes into sharp focus.

When we finally step away from the relationship, the absence of this constant stimulation is difficult for your brain to adapt to.

The peace you once longed for suddenly feels foreign. The contrast between the chaos of the relationship and the relative quiet of being alone can make everything feel disorienting. Your nervous system, used to the heightened tension and drama, is now searching for a new balance, leaving you with feelings of emptiness, confusion, and sometimes even guilt.

Even after significant time has passed, it is possible to find ourselves unexpectedly triggered by something related to the past relationship. We may fixate on unresolved conflicts, things that still feel unfinished or hurtful. These unresolved issues create emotional knots that we didn't fully untangle while we were still in the relationship. They can now come rushing to the surface when least expected, leaving us feeling blindsided, as if the trauma has never really left.

What we're feeling is not a regression; it's a process of emotional release. It's natural to feel like we're back in the chaos of the breakup, even if time has passed. The feelings of confusion, frustration, and anger that you are experiencing now may feel even more intense than when you were in the relationship because there is no longer a specific place for those emotions to go. When you were in the relationship, you were engaged in a constant push-pull dynamic that kept your emotions in motion. Now that the relationship is over, the emotions are no longer directed toward resolving conflict; instead, they are free-floating, lingering in your mind and body.

One of the most perplexing aspects of post-breakup trauma is the unpredictability of when emotional upheaval will strike. We may feel fine for weeks, months, or even longer, only to be blindsided by intense feelings of loss, anger, or betrayal months or even a year after the relationship ended. It may seem irrational to feel such intensity after so much time, and yet, it's part of the healing process.

Triggers can be anything: an unexpected encounter with our ex, seeing them with someone new, hearing a song that reminds us of the past, or even something as simple as a specific smell. These triggers can pull us back into a state of confusion as if we are reliving the pain of the breakup all over again.

If we find ourselve consumed by anger, confusion, or sadness, it is essential to recognize that these feelings are part of the healing process. we are not regressing; rather, we are confronting and processing trauma that was never fully dealt with during the relationship. It's crucial to show compassion toward ourselve during this time. Understand that what we are feeling is valid and normal, and that it is a natural consequence of having been in a high-stress, emotionally taxing situation.

As you work through your emotions, take care to avoid destructive behaviors that might deepen your sense of pain. It's easy to fall into cycles of self-blame, anger, or bitterness, but these emotions can only prolong your suffering. Instead, try to focus on taking small steps toward healing. Practice self-care, reach out to supportive friends or a therapist, and allow yourself to express your feelings without judgment. The more we recognize that these emotional outbursts are part of our natural healing process, the easier it will become to navigate them.

Eventually, this intense emotional period will pass. With time and self-compassion, we will find our way back to emotional stability. The key is to understand that we are not broken, nor are we failing. The emotional rollercoaster we're experiencing is a testament to our resilience, not our inability to heal. By acknowledging the connection between our current emotional state and the trauma of the past, we can empower ourselves to move forward.

The journey of healing from a tumultuous relationship is not linear. There will be setbacks, but with each setback comes growth. The most important thing is to allow ourselves the time and space to heal at our own pace, without rushing the process. Every tear shed, every moment of anger, and every wave of sadness is a step toward resolution. The emotional turbulence will eventually subside, leaving you stronger, more self-aware, and better equipped for the relationships that lie ahead.
When you lose hope just remember what Krishna said in chapter 4 shlok 11

ये यथा मां प्रपद्यन्ते तांस्तथैव भजाम्यहम्।

everyone surrenders to me and I reward them accordingly.

"It's better to live alone than to be with someone and alone"

www.ingramcontent.com/pod-product-compliance
Lightning Source LLC
Chambersburg PA
CBHW050022170726
48282CB00025B/503
* 9 7 8 9 3 6 6 3 1 3 6 4 1 *